JOSH STEVE

Echoes of Eternity

Copyright © 2023 by Josh Steve

All rights reserved. No part of this publication may be reproduced, stored or transmitted in any form or by any means, electronic, mechanical, photocopying, recording, scanning, or otherwise without written permission from the publisher. It is illegal to copy this book, post it to a website, or distribute it by any other means without permission.

First edition

This book was professionally typeset on Reedsy. Find out more at reedsy.com

Contents

Mysterious Artifact	1
Cryptic Clues	4
Forbidden Archives	7
Pursuit Begins	12
The Enigmatic Guardian	17
The Legacy of the Eternal Echo	25
The Echoes Resonate	31
Whispers of Destiny	39
The Relics Awaken	48
The Echoes Resonate	55
The Symphony of Resonance	60
The Symphony's Legacy	65

Mysterious Artifact

Dr. Elizabeth Morgan stood in the dimly lit basement of the dusty old museum, surrounded by towering shelves laden with forgotten relics of history. Her eyes scanned the rows of artifacts, but one peculiar item had captured her attention—a small, unassuming wooden box adorned with intricate carvings. It sat alone on a plain pedestal, as if beckoning her to uncover its secrets.

The box's origins were shrouded in mystery. It had been discovered in the ruins of an ancient temple deep within a remote jungle, hidden away from prying eyes for centuries. Dr. Morgan, a renowned historian with a passion for unraveling the past, had been granted access to this enigmatic artifact by a reclusive collector who believed it held the key to an untold history.

As she approached the box, her gloved hand reached out to trace the intricate designs etched into the wood. The carvings depicted scenes of celestial bodies, intricate constellations, and cryptic symbols that defied any known language. It was a puzzle begging to be solved.

Her breath quickened with excitement and trepidation. This was the moment she had been waiting for—a chance to unlock a forgotten chapter of history. Her heart pounded as she gently lifted the lid of the box. Inside, nestled within a bed of velvet, lay a small, ornate key and a parchment bearing unfamiliar writing.

Elizabeth carefully retrieved the key, noting its exquisite craftsmanship. She turned her attention to the parchment, its aged paper brittle and fragile. The writing was unlike anything she had ever seen before—a script that seemed to dance across the page, its meaning eluding her grasp.

With a sense of determination, she took a deep breath and began to decipher the cryptic text. Hours passed as she poured over ancient dictionaries and reference books, comparing symbols and cross-referencing obscure texts. Her eyes strained, her mind raced, and the mystery deepened.

It was well into the night when Elizabeth finally made a breakthrough. The writing on the parchment seemed to describe a hidden location, one that had remained concealed for centuries. It spoke of an underground chamber, a place of immense importance, and it hinted at the existence of an ancient secret society sworn to protect this knowledge.

The implications of her discovery sent shivers down her spine. Elizabeth knew she was treading on dangerous ground, but her thirst for knowledge outweighed her fear. She had to find this hidden chamber and uncover the truth behind the artifact.

She glanced at the clock on the wall; its hands pointed to 2:00 AM. Exhaustion tugged at her, but there was no time for sleep. With the newfound knowledge burning in her mind, she gathered her belongings, carefully stowing the key and the parchment in her bag. The artifact had opened a door to a world of secrets, and she was determined to step through it.

As she made her way out of the museum, the echoing footsteps in the empty corridors seemed to mock her. She couldn't shake the feeling that she was being watched, that the discovery of the box had set events into motion beyond her control.

Little did she know that her journey into the echoes of eternity had only just begun. The mysterious artifact had marked her as a player in a game of history, secrets, and danger that would challenge everything she thought she knew and test the limits of her courage and resolve.

Cryptic Clues

The pale morning light crept through the curtains of Dr. Elizabeth Morgan's cramped apartment, revealing a room filled with books and maps, a testament to her lifelong pursuit of history's hidden enigmas. She had spent the restless night pondering the parchment's cryptic message, the words swirling in her mind like riddles demanding answers.

With newfound determination, she spread the parchment across her cluttered desk, its symbols illuminated by the soft glow of her desk lamp. The translation she had painstakingly deciphered beckoned her to an undisclosed location—a place hinted at but never marked on any known map.

As Elizabeth traced her fingers over the mysterious writing, her thoughts wandered to the secret society mentioned in the text. Who were they, and what role had they played in safeguarding this enigma for centuries? She knew she couldn't embark on this quest alone. Her curiosity was a fire burning within her, but so was the sense of foreboding.

Summoning her courage, Elizabeth decided to seek guidance from a trusted friend and fellow historian, Professor Daniel Ramirez. They had shared many a late night deciphering ancient scripts and chasing history's elusive whispers together. She trusted him with her life and knew he would understand the gravity of her discovery.

With a sense of urgency, Elizabeth dialed Daniel's number, her fingers trembling slightly as she waited for him to pick up. After a few rings, his voice crackled through the phone.

"Elizabeth? It's quite early," Daniel yawned, his voice thick with sleep.

"Daniel, I need your help," Elizabeth replied, her words laced with urgency.

Intrigued by her tone, Daniel instantly snapped to attention. "What's happened?"

"I've stumbled upon something incredible," she began, recounting the discovery of the mysterious artifact, the cryptic message, and the potential existence of a hidden chamber. "I can't do this alone, Daniel. I need your expertise."

There was a moment of silence on the other end of the line before Daniel spoke. "Meet me at the usual place in an hour."

Relief washed over Elizabeth as she hung up the phone. She knew Daniel wouldn't hesitate to join her in this quest for knowledge and adventure. She quickly packed the parchment, the key, and her notes, ensuring they were secure. Time was of the essence.

As she made her way to their meeting spot, a small, dimly lit café tucked away in a quiet corner of the city, Elizabeth couldn't shake the feeling that they were stepping into a world of danger and intrigue. Her mind raced with questions about the key, the hidden chamber, and the elusive secret society. What had they guarded for centuries, and why was it so vital that it remained hidden?

The café was nearly empty when Elizabeth arrived, save for a few early morning patrons sipping their coffee in solitude. She spotted Daniel sitting in a corner booth, his salt-and-pepper hair and glasses lending him an air of scholarly wisdom. He glanced up as she approached, a knowing look in his eyes.

"Daniel," she greeted him, sliding into the seat across from him.

"Elizabeth," he replied, his voice low and serious. "Tell me everything."

For the next hour, Elizabeth poured out the details of her discovery, from the artifact to the cryptic message to her late-night research. Daniel listened intently, occasionally jotting down notes on a small notepad.

When she finished, he leaned back in his seat, his fingers steepled in thought. "This is unlike anything we've ever encountered," he said. "It's as if we've stumbled upon a hidden thread in the fabric of history."

"I know," Elizabeth agreed, her eyes filled with a mixture of excitement and trepidation. "But we need to find this hidden chamber. The parchment's message hints at its location, but it's cryptic. We may need to follow the clues it provides."

Daniel nodded, his expression determined. "We'll start by deciphering the message further, cross-referencing it with historical records and maps. If there's any hint of its whereabouts, we'll find it."

As they made plans to embark on this perilous journey together, neither of them could have anticipated the challenges, mysteries, and dangers that awaited them in the quest for the hidden chamber. The enigmatic artifact and its cryptic message had set them on a path where history and the present collided, and their pursuit of the truth would plunge them into a world of secrets and suspense beyond their wildest imaginations.

Forbidden Archives

The days blurred into nights as Dr. Elizabeth Morgan and Professor Daniel Ramirez delved deeper into their quest to decipher the cryptic message from the mysterious artifact. Their shared excitement was palpable, an unquenchable thirst for knowledge driving them forward. But with every step they took, the shadows of danger and intrigue grew longer.

Their research led them to the hallowed halls of the National Archives, a sprawling repository of historical documents and records. It was a place they had visited countless times before, but this time, it held the promise of unveiling secrets hidden for centuries.

As they entered the grand building, its marble floors echoing with the hushed voices of historians and researchers, Elizabeth couldn't help but feel a sense of awe. The National Archives held an immense wealth of knowledge, and today, they were here to uncover a piece of that knowledge that had eluded everyone else.

"Where do we begin?" Daniel asked, his eyes scanning the vast expanse of shelves that stretched before them.

Elizabeth produced the parchment with the cryptic message. "We start by cross-referencing these symbols with any historical texts, maps, or references we can find. We need to determine if there's any mention of the location or the secret society."

They spent hours poring over ancient manuscripts, crumbling maps, and dusty records. The symbols on the parchment seemed to be a language unto themselves, defying easy translation. Their fingers traced the intricate patterns, trying to discern any recurring shapes or patterns.

The archivists and librarians watched them with curious eyes, noting their intense focus and whispered conversations. Elizabeth and Daniel had always been dedicated scholars, but today, they were on a different kind of mission—one that transcended academia.

As the afternoon sun cast long shadows across the archives, Elizabeth's eyes widened. She had found something—a map from the 17th century, depicting a remote region deep within a dense forest. The markings on the map seemed to match some of the symbols on the parchment.

"Daniel, look at this," she said, excitement bubbling within her.

He leaned over her shoulder, studying the map. "It's a place called 'The Whispering Grove.' It matches some of the symbols on the parchment."

Elizabeth's heart raced. "Could this be it? Could this be the location the parchment is referring to?"

"It's possible," Daniel replied, his voice tinged with anticipation. "But we need to find out more about this 'Whispering Grove' and its significance."

They continued their research, unearthing old diaries and journals of explorers who had ventured into the dense forest where the Whispering Grove was rumored to be located. The entries were cryptic, hinting at strange phenomena and encounters with an elusive secret society.

Hours turned into days as they pieced together a fragmented history. It appeared that the Whispering Grove had been a sacred site for an ancient order, a place where they gathered to conduct mysterious ceremonies and protect an enigmatic treasure. But what was this treasure, and why had it been hidden away for so long?

Their research was abruptly interrupted when a stern-faced archivist approached them. "I'm afraid this is as far as you can go," he said, eyeing them with suspicion.

Elizabeth and Daniel exchanged uneasy glances. "We're just conducting historical research," Elizabeth explained, trying to keep her voice steady.

The archivist's gaze bore into them. "There are some documents that are off-limits, restricted to certain individuals."

Daniel spoke up, his tone measured. "We understand, but we believe that this information is of great historical importance. It's our duty to uncover it."

The archivist hesitated, torn between duty and curiosity. Finally, he relented. "Follow me."

They were led through a labyrinthine series of corridors until they reached a door marked "Restricted Archives." The archivist unlocked it, revealing a room bathed in dim, golden light, lined with shelves of leather-bound volumes and ancient scrolls.

"This is as far as you can go," the archivist warned, leaving them to their research.

As they delved into the restricted archives, Elizabeth's heart raced. They had access to information that few had ever seen. The documents revealed that the Whispering Grove had been a site of great power, where the secret society had conducted rituals to safeguard a relic known as the "Eternal Echo."

The nature of the Eternal Echo remained shrouded in mystery, but it was said to hold the power to unlock hidden knowledge and manipulate time itself. It was both a blessing and a curse, capable of great good or immense destruction in the wrong hands.

The more they uncovered, the more dangerous their quest became. They had stumbled upon something that had remained hidden for centuries, something that powerful individuals and organizations would stop at nothing to possess.

As they continued to research, a series of ominous events unfolded. They received anonymous threats, warning them to abandon their quest. Their phones were tapped, and their movements were surveilled. It was clear that someone did not want them to uncover the truth.

One evening, as they left the National Archives, they were ambushed by shadowy figures in the dimly lit alleyway. It was a desperate struggle, but Elizabeth and Daniel managed to escape with their lives, bruised and battered, their determination only hardened by the danger they faced.

"We can't give up now," Daniel declared as they huddled in the safety of Elizabeth's apartment. "We're on the brink of uncovering something extraordinary, something that could change history."

Elizabeth nodded, her eyes reflecting both fear and determination. "We'll need to be even more cautious and resourceful from now on. The secrets of the Whispering Grove must be revealed, and the truth of the Eternal Echo must be understood."

With the threat of danger looming over them and the weight of history's mysteries upon their shoulders, Elizabeth and Daniel continued their relentless pursuit of the truth, unaware that their journey into the echoes of eternity had only just begun. The cryptic symbols, the hidden location, and the enigmatic secret society were all pieces of a puzzle that would test the limits of their intellect, courage, and resolve.

Pursuit Begins

The events of the past weeks had left Dr. Elizabeth Morgan and Professor Daniel Ramirez on edge, their lives transformed into a dangerous game of pursuit and evasion. As they continued to unravel the mysteries surrounding the Whispering Grove and the elusive secret society, the shadows that clung to their every step grew darker.

It was a moonless night when Elizabeth received a cryptic message on her encrypted phone, a message that sent shivers down her spine. The sender remained anonymous, but the words were chillingly clear: "Stop digging, or there will be consequences."

She immediately showed the message to Daniel, her voice trembling with unease. "They know we're onto something, Daniel. They're trying to scare us away."

He studied the message carefully. "We can't let fear dictate our actions. This quest has become too important, too significant. We have to press on."

With renewed determination, they returned to their research, determined to discover the truth behind the Eternal Echo and the secret society that had guarded it for centuries. But the threats did not end with the message; they were merely the beginning.

One evening, as they were leaving the National Archives, a dark sedan pulled up alongside them. The windows were tinted, concealing the occupants, but the message was clear. A chilling voice emanated from the car's speakers, distorted and ominous.

"Dr. Morgan, Professor Ramirez, you're meddling in matters that don't concern you. Leave this path now, or you will regret it."

Elizabeth's heart pounded as she clutched Daniel's arm, her voice defiant. "Who are you? What do you want?"

The car sped away without a word, leaving them shaken and unsettled. It was clear that their adversaries were not to be underestimated, and the danger was escalating.

They decided to take precautions, investing in state-of-the-art encryption for their communications and changing their daily routines to evade surveillance. Yet, they couldn't shake the feeling of being watched, of being hunted.

One evening, as Elizabeth returned to her apartment after a day of research, she noticed that her door was ajar. Panic surged through her veins as she cautiously pushed it open, her senses alert. The apartment appeared undisturbed, but something was amiss—a sense of intrusion that left her on edge.

Daniel arrived soon after, and together, they combed through the apartment, searching for any signs of unauthorized entry. It was then that they discovered it—their research notes scattered across the floor, their belongings rifled through, and the parchment with the cryptic message was missing.

"Someone was here," Elizabeth whispered, her voice trembling with a mixture of fear and anger.

"They took the parchment," Daniel confirmed, his jaw clenched. "We're dealing with someone who wants this information as badly as we do."

Their quest had become a race against time. They needed to recover the stolen parchment and decipher its remaining clues before their enemies could unlock the secrets of the Whispering Grove and the Eternal Echo. The implications of failure were too dire to contemplate.

The next day, they embarked on a desperate search for their stolen research. Their pursuit led them to a seedy underground bar on the outskirts of the city, a place where whispers of shadowy dealings and covert meetings abounded. They had received a tip that the stolen parchment might be there.

As they entered the dimly lit establishment, the air thick with the scent of alcohol and tension, they attracted curious glances from the patrons. It was clear they didn't belong, and that only heightened the danger of their mission.

They discreetly approached the bartender, a burly man with a scarred face who eyed them warily. Elizabeth slipped a photograph of the stolen parchment across the bar, her voice low and urgent. "Have you seen this? We're willing to pay for information."

The bartender studied the photograph before shaking his head. "I ain't seen nothin' like that. You best be leavin.'"

They left the bar, their hopes dashed. It had been a long shot, but they couldn't afford to give up. As they stepped out into the night, a sudden sense of foreboding washed over them. They knew they were being followed.

They quickened their pace, weaving through the labyrinthine streets of the city, but their pursuers were relentless. It was a harrowing game of cat and mouse, their breaths labored, their hearts pounding. As they turned a corner, they found themselves trapped in a narrow alley, their escape cut off.

The figures closing in on them wore dark suits and masks, their identities concealed. It was a silent confrontation, a standoff in the shadows.

"Give us the information you've uncovered," one of them demanded, his voice cold and unyielding.

Elizabeth and Daniel exchanged a determined look. "We won't be intimidated," Elizabeth replied, her voice steady. "The secrets we seek belong to history, not to those who would use them for nefarious purposes."

The tension in the alley grew palpable, and just when it seemed like a confrontation was inevitable, a deafening crash echoed from above. Bricks and debris rained down upon the masked figures, sending them scrambling for cover.

Elizabeth and Daniel seized the opportunity to escape, their hearts pounding with adrenaline. They didn't know who had come to their rescue, but they were grateful for the timely intervention.

They returned to the safety of Elizabeth's apartment, their stolen research still elusive, but their determination unbroken. It was clear that their quest had drawn the attention of powerful and dangerous adversaries, but they couldn't turn back now.

"We're running out of time," Daniel said, his voice tinged with urgency. "We need to decipher the remaining clues on our own and recover the stolen parchment."

Elizabeth nodded, her eyes reflecting determination and defiance. "We'll find the Whispering Grove, and we'll unlock the secrets of the Eternal Echo. No matter what it takes."

With their backs against the wall, pursued by unseen enemies, Elizabeth and

Daniel continued their relentless pursuit of the truth, determined to uncover the mysteries that had remained hidden for centuries. The stolen parchment was a puzzle piece they couldn't afford to lose, and their quest would test the limits of their courage, resourcefulness, and resilience. The echoes of eternity called to them, and they would not rest until they had answered that haunting call.

The Enigmatic Guardian

The stolen parchment remained elusive, and the threats that loomed over Dr. Elizabeth Morgan and Professor Daniel Ramirez grew more ominous with each passing day. But their relentless pursuit of the mysteries surrounding the Whispering Grove and the Eternal Echo remained undeterred. They knew that the answers lay hidden, waiting to be uncovered.

In their quest to decipher the remaining clues on the parchment, Elizabeth and Daniel revisited their notes and research. The symbols and cryptic writings seemed to taunt them, their meaning just beyond their grasp. They needed a breakthrough, a revelation that would lead them closer to their goal.

As they sat in Elizabeth's apartment, a disheartening sense of frustration settled upon them. The stolen parchment was a key piece of the puzzle, and without it, they were navigating a labyrinth in the dark.

"We can't give up," Daniel insisted, his voice filled with determination. "We have to find another way, another source of information."

Elizabeth nodded, her mind racing. "Perhaps we should focus on the Whispering Grove itself. If we can uncover its history and significance, it might lead us to the Eternal Echo."

With renewed purpose, they turned their attention to the Whispering Grove. Historical records and maps hinted at its location within a remote, dense forest, but the specifics remained elusive. They decided to consult experts in ancient cartography, hoping to uncover hidden maps or references that had been overlooked.

Their search led them to an elderly cartographer named Samuel Hawthorne, a recluse known for his expertise in deciphering obscure maps and locating lost landmarks. It took weeks of persuasion and cajoling, but Samuel finally agreed to meet with them.

In a dimly lit room cluttered with maps and charts, Samuel examined the photographs and notes Elizabeth and Daniel had brought. His fingers traced the symbols on the parchment, his eyes narrowing in concentration.

"The Whispering Grove," he mused, his voice a low rumble. "A place lost to time and memory. It's said to be hidden deep within the heart of the forest, but its location has been shrouded in secrecy for centuries."

"Can you help us find it?" Elizabeth asked, her voice hopeful.

Samuel leaned back in his creaking chair, his expression contemplative. "I can provide you with a map, a map that has been passed down through generations of cartographers in my family. It contains clues that may lead you to the Whispering Grove."

Their excitement surged as Samuel retrieved an ancient-looking map from a locked cabinet. The parchment was yellowed with age, its ink faded, but the markings were intricate and detailed. It depicted a portion of the forest, complete with landmarks, trails, and a winding river.

"This map holds the key to the Whispering Grove," Samuel said, his voice hushed. "But I must warn you, the forest is treacherous, and the journey will not be easy."

Elizabeth and Daniel exchanged determined glances. "We're willing to take that risk," Daniel replied.

Before they left, Samuel offered a final piece of advice. "Beware of those who seek the same secrets. The guardian of the Whispering Grove is as enigmatic as the secrets it holds. Trust no one but yourselves."

Armed with the ancient map and a renewed sense of purpose, Elizabeth and Daniel ventured into the wilderness. They followed the map's intricate directions, navigating dense underbrush and steep terrain. The forest seemed to close in around them, the silence broken only by the rustle of leaves and the distant murmur of the river.

As they journeyed deeper into the forest, they encountered strange phenomena—whispers in the wind, eerie glows in the underbrush, and the feeling of being watched. It was as if the forest itself was alive, guarding its secrets with a sinister vigilance.

Days turned into weeks as they pressed on, guided by the map's cryptic markings. They faced challenges that tested their resolve—treacherous ravines, thunderstorms, and encounters with elusive wildlife. But they refused to be deterred, their determination unshaken.

One evening, as they made camp by a babbling brook, a soft melody filled the air. It was a haunting tune, ethereal and otherworldly. Elizabeth and Daniel exchanged puzzled glances, their senses on high alert.

The melody drew them deeper into the forest, leading them to a clearing bathed in moonlight. In the center of the clearing stood a figure, cloaked in shadows, their features concealed. The melody emanated from this enigmatic guardian, a tune that seemed to resonate with the very essence of the Whispering Grove.

Elizabeth and Daniel approached cautiously, their hearts pounding. The guardian's voice, when they finally spoke, was a melodic whisper that echoed through the clearing.

"You seek the secrets of the Whispering Grove," the guardian intoned, their words cryptic and laden with ancient wisdom.

"We do," Elizabeth replied, her voice steady. "We seek the Eternal Echo and the knowledge that has been hidden for centuries."

The guardian regarded them with eyes that seemed to pierce their souls. "The secrets of the Whispering Grove are not easily revealed. They are protected by the spirits of the forest, by the very essence of time itself."

"We understand," Daniel said, his voice filled with reverence. "But we must uncover the truth, for the sake of history and knowledge."

The guardian's melody swelled, filling the clearing with an ethereal resonance. "Very well, seekers of truth. To unlock the secrets of the Whispering Grove, you must prove your worthiness. You must undergo the Trial of Echoes."

With those words, the guardian's form dissolved into mist, merging with the very air around them. The forest seemed to come alive, its ancient trees whispering secrets, its leaves dancing in a spectral ballet. Elizabeth and Daniel were enveloped in a surreal world, a realm where time and reality blurred.

The Trial of Echoes was a journey through the annals of history, a test of their knowledge, their courage, and their resolve. They witnessed pivotal moments in time, reliving the past and glimpsing the future. They encountered figures from history, each offering cryptic clues and challenges.

Days turned into weeks within this surreal realm, but Elizabeth and Daniel pressed on, determined to overcome the Trial of Echoes and unlock the secrets they sought. They faced impossible odds, tested the limits of their intellect, and delved into the deepest recesses of their souls.

Finally, after what felt like an eternity, they stood before the guardian once more, their spirits weary but unbroken.

"You have proven your worthiness," the guardian intoned. "The Whispering Grove shall reveal its secrets to you."

With a wave of the guardian's hand, the forest seemed to part, revealing a hidden chamber bathed in a soft, otherworldly light. It was a place of immense significance, a place where the secrets of the Eternal Echo lay waiting to be discovered.

As Elizabeth and Daniel stepped into the chamber, they felt the weight of history and the echoes of eternity surrounding them. The culmination of their journey had brought them to this pivotal moment, a moment that would change the course of their lives and the fate of the knowledge they sought to uncover.

With bated breath and hearts filled with anticipation, they ventured further into the chamber, ready to unveil the mysteries that had remained hidden for centuries. The echoes of eternity beckoned them, and they were determined to answer that haunting call.

The chamber's interior was a breathtaking tableau of history and secrets. Ancient artifacts and relics adorned shelves, their presence adding to the air of mystique that hung in the chamber. At its center lay a pedestal upon which rested an ornate, intricately designed chest. It was the culmination of their journey—the key to unlocking the Eternal Echo.

With trembling hands, Elizabeth and Daniel approached the chest. Its carvings and symbols were reminiscent of those on the stolen parchment. It was a testament to the ancient order's skill and craftsmanship.

As they unlocked the chest with the key they had carried with them throughout their journey, a soft, melodic hum filled the chamber. The lid slowly creaked open, revealing a collection of scrolls and manuscripts, each adorned with the same cryptic symbols that had led them here.

These documents were the culmination of centuries of knowledge, a repository of secrets that had been guarded with utmost devotion. Elizabeth and Daniel recognized the symbols, but their meaning remained a puzzle. They began the arduous task of translating and deciphering the texts, knowing that the answers they sought were buried within.

The guardian, now manifesting as a spectral presence, watched over them as they worked. Time seemed to warp in the chamber, and they lost track of hours, immersed in the task at hand. The texts revealed the history of the Eternal Echo, its power, and the responsibility of those who had protected it.

It was said that the Eternal Echo held the memories of the world, an archive of knowledge that could unveil the truths of the past and the future. But its power was a double-edged sword, capable of great good or unimaginable destruction.

As they delved deeper into the texts, they uncovered references to the secret society that had guarded the Eternal Echo—the Guardians of Eternity. This society had been formed by the ancient scholars who had discovered the relic's existence, dedicated to ensuring it remained hidden and protected from those who would misuse it.

Elizabeth and Daniel marveled at the dedication of these scholars, who had devoted their lives to the preservation of knowledge. It was a legacy that they now carried, the weight of history and the secrets of the Whispering Grove resting upon their shoulders.

But their discovery was not without its consequences. The chamber's guardians had entrusted them with the knowledge of the Eternal Echo, but they were also aware that their quest had drawn the attention of those who sought to exploit its power.

As they prepared to leave the chamber, the guardian's spectral presence spoke once more. "You now hold the knowledge of the Eternal Echo. Use it wisely, for its power is both a gift and a burden. Guard it as the Guardians of Eternity once did."

With those words, the guardian's presence dissipated, leaving them alone in the chamber. They carefully gathered the translated texts and manuscripts, knowing that they carried with them the weight of history and the responsibility of preserving the secrets they had uncovered.

The journey back through the forest was as treacherous as their arrival, but they emerged from the wilderness changed, their spirits tempered by the knowledge they now possessed. The Eternal Echo was no longer a mystery, but a legacy to be protected and shared.

Their return to civilization was met with mixed emotions. They were relieved to have uncovered the secrets of the Whispering Grove, but they were acutely aware that their adversaries still sought the power of the Eternal Echo. They had become custodians of a precious legacy, and they would need to be vigilant in safeguarding it.

With the translated texts in their possession, Elizabeth and Daniel resumed their research, determined to understand the true extent of the Eternal Echo's capabilities. It was a task that would require time, dedication, and collaboration with experts from various fields.

As they delved into the texts, their discoveries began to unfold—a glimpse into the past, the future, and the echoes of eternity. They realized that the

Eternal Echo had the power to shape history, to reveal the untold stories of civilizations long gone, and to shed light on the mysteries of the cosmos.

But they also understood the danger that came with this knowledge, the potential for misuse and destruction. The responsibility of wielding the power of the Eternal Echo weighed heavily on their shoulders.

As the days turned into weeks and the weeks into months, Elizabeth and Daniel continued their research, their quest for knowledge and the preservation of history ever at the forefront of their minds. They knew that their journey was far from over, that the secrets they had uncovered were only the beginning of a new chapter in their lives.

The whispers of the forest, the haunting melody of the guardian, and the enigmatic power of the Eternal Echo would forever linger in their memories, a reminder of the extraordinary journey they had undertaken in the pursuit of truth. They had answered the echoes of eternity, and in doing so, had become guardians of a legacy that transcended time itself.

The Legacy of the Eternal Echo

It was a crisp, clear morning in late September when Dr. Elizabeth Morgan and Professor Daniel Ramirez returned to the hallowed halls of the National Archives. The warmth of summer had given way to the cool embrace of autumn, and the changing leaves painted the city in a tapestry of reds and golds.

They had spent months poring over the translated texts and manuscripts they had uncovered in the Whispering Grove, seeking to understand the true extent of the Eternal Echo's power. The secrets they had unearthed were both awe-inspiring and humbling, and they knew that the time had come to share their discoveries with the world.

The National Archives, with its imposing neoclassical facade, seemed to beckon them inside, as if it held the key to unlocking the next chapter of their journey. As they entered the grand building, the archivists and librarians greeted them with knowing smiles, aware of the significance of their quest.

Elizabeth and Daniel had requested a private meeting with the Director of the National Archives, a distinguished historian named Professor Amelia Hawthorne. She was renowned for her scholarship and her dedication to preserving the secrets of history. It was to her that they intended to reveal the truth about the Eternal Echo.

They were led through a maze of corridors until they reached Professor

Hawthorne's office—a spacious room adorned with bookshelves that reached the ceiling, filled with volumes of knowledge spanning centuries. She sat behind an antique desk, her silver hair gleaming in the soft light that filtered through the window.

"Dr. Morgan, Professor Ramirez, please have a seat," she said, gesturing to the chairs before her desk.

They took their seats, their hearts pounding with anticipation. Elizabeth spoke first, her voice steady but filled with reverence. "Professor Hawthorne, we come before you today to share a discovery of profound significance—one that has the power to reshape our understanding of history."

Daniel continued, his words measured and resolute. "We have uncovered the secrets of the Whispering Grove and the Eternal Echo—a relic that holds the memories of the world, a repository of knowledge that spans the ages."

Professor Hawthorne regarded them with a mixture of curiosity and intrigue. "You have my full attention. Please, proceed."

They began to reveal the knowledge they had uncovered—the history of the Eternal Echo, its power to reveal the truths of the past and the future, and the responsibility of those who had protected it. They recounted their journey through the Trial of Echoes and the guardian of the Whispering Grove, emphasizing the importance of safeguarding this legacy.

As they spoke, Professor Hawthorne's expression shifted from curiosity to amazement, her eyes widening with each revelation. She listened intently, absorbing the weight of their words.

When they had finished, there was a profound silence in the room, as if the very air had stilled in reverence for the knowledge shared. Professor Hawthorne finally spoke, her voice filled with wonder. "This is a revelation of unparalleled significance. The Eternal Echo is a treasure that must be preserved and shared with the world."

"We believe the same," Elizabeth replied. "But we also understand the dangers that come with this knowledge. There are those who would seek to exploit its power."

Professor Hawthorne nodded in agreement. "Indeed, the responsibility of safeguarding the Eternal Echo is a grave one. It must be protected from those who would misuse it, and its secrets must be shared with scholars and historians dedicated to preserving the truth."

With that, a plan began to take shape—a plan to create a consortium of scholars and historians who would serve as custodians of the Eternal Echo. They would be entrusted with the responsibility of studying and preserving its knowledge, while ensuring that it remained shielded from those who sought to exploit it.

The process of forming the consortium was a meticulous one. They reached out to experts from various fields—historians, archaeologists, linguists, and philosophers—individuals who shared a deep reverence for history and a commitment to the preservation of knowledge.

Months passed as the consortium took shape, with each member contributing their expertise to the cause. They established a secure location to house the Eternal Echo's documents, a place hidden from prying eyes but accessible to those deemed worthy.

The unveiling of the consortium was met with great anticipation in academic circles and among historians worldwide. The National Archives became its official headquarters, and its members worked tirelessly to catalog, translate, and study the contents of the Eternal Echo.

As the consortium's activities gained momentum, Elizabeth and Daniel remained at the forefront, their journey far from over. They continued to uncover hidden truths and lost histories, delving into the wealth of knowledge stored within the Eternal Echo.

The power of the relic was not lost on them, and they approached its study with reverence and caution. They discovered lost civilizations, untold stories of heroes and heroines, and the secrets of ancient sciences and philosophies.

But they also uncovered the darker aspects of history—the atrocities committed, the injustices endured, and the lessons that should never be forgotten. The Eternal Echo held within it the collective memory of humanity, a mirror reflecting the triumphs and tragedies of the past.

One evening, as Elizabeth and Daniel sat in the consortium's study room, bathed in the warm glow of lamplight, they discussed the responsibility they bore. The weight of history and the echoes of eternity rested upon their shoulders.

"We must ensure that the knowledge we uncover is used for the betterment of humanity," Elizabeth said, her voice filled with conviction. "The lessons of the past must guide us toward a brighter future."

Daniel nodded in agreement. "We have the power to shape how this knowledge is shared and understood. It's a tremendous responsibility, but one we cannot shirk."

Their commitment to preserving the legacy of the Eternal Echo remained unwavering, and they worked tirelessly to ensure that the consortium's activities aligned with their values. They established guidelines for responsible research and ethical use of the knowledge within the relic.

As the years passed, the consortium flourished, its membership expanding to include scholars and historians from around the world. The study of the Eternal Echo became a respected field of research, and its revelations continued to enrich humanity's understanding of its own history.

But their journey was not without challenges. There were those who sought to exploit the Eternal Echo for personal gain or nefarious purposes. The consortium's security measures had to be continually strengthened, and its members remained vigilant in protecting the relic.

In the midst of their scholarly pursuits, Elizabeth and Daniel's bond deepened. Their shared experiences, their dedication to the consortium, and their reverence for history had forged a connection that transcended the ordinary. It was a love that had grown quietly amidst the echoes of eternity, a love that they chose to nurture and cherish.

One evening, as they stood on the rooftop of the National Archives, gazing out at the city bathed in the golden light of sunset, Daniel took Elizabeth's hand in his. "Elizabeth," he began, his voice tender, "our journey has been filled with challenges and revelations. But it has also brought us closer than I ever imagined."

She turned to him, her eyes reflecting the warmth of the setting sun. "Daniel, our love has been woven into the fabric of our quest, a love that has grown amidst the echoes of eternity."

He smiled, his gaze unwavering. "Will you do me the honor of sharing the rest of our journey together, as partners in life and in the preservation of history?"

Tears welled in Elizabeth's eyes as she nodded. "Yes, Daniel, a thousand times yes."

Their love story was a testament to the enduring power of shared passion and purpose. They were united not only by their love for each other but also by their commitment to safeguarding the knowledge of the Eternal Echo for future generations.

In the years that followed, they married in a quiet ceremony attended by their fellow consortium members, who had become their closest friends and allies. Their love story became legendary among scholars, a symbol of the enduring connection between history and humanity.

As they stood on the rooftop, hand in hand, they knew that their journey was far from over. The echoes of eternity continued to call to them, whispering secrets that had yet to be uncovered. They faced the future with a sense of purpose and determination, ready to embrace the challenges and revelations that lay ahead.

And so, Dr. Elizabeth Morgan and Professor Daniel Ramirez continued their quest, guardians of the Eternal Echo and custodians of history's legacy. They walked hand in hand into the unknown, their love and dedication lighting the path for generations to come.

In the end, their story was not just about the pursuit of knowledge or the preservation of history; it was a testament to the enduring power of the human spirit, the echoes of eternity that bound us all, and the love that transcended time itself.

The Echoes Resonate

In the heart of winter, when frost painted delicate patterns on the windows of the National Archives, the members of the consortium gathered once more. It had been several years since Dr. Elizabeth Morgan and Professor Daniel Ramirez had revealed the secrets of the Eternal Echo, and the relic had become an invaluable source of knowledge, guiding historians and scholars in their quest to uncover the hidden truths of the past.

The consortium's study room, with its oak-paneled walls and towering bookshelves, was abuzz with activity. Scholars from around the world had convened to share their findings, their excitement palpable as they discussed the latest revelations uncovered within the Eternal Echo.

Among the consortium members was a young historian named Emily Turner, whose fascination with history had led her to join the group. She had been mentored by Elizabeth and Daniel, and her dedication to the study of the relic had quickly earned her a place of respect among her peers.

As the discussions continued, Emily couldn't help but feel a sense of awe at the wealth of knowledge that surrounded her. The Eternal Echo had become a beacon of enlightenment, a source of inspiration for all who sought to understand the past and its impact on the present.

Elizabeth and Daniel, now seasoned scholars in their own right, presided over the meeting with a sense of pride and fulfillment. Their journey, which had begun in the shadows of the Whispering Grove, had led them to this moment—a moment where history came alive, and the echoes of eternity resonated in the hearts and minds of those gathered.

But amidst the scholarly discussions and the camaraderie of the consortium, a sense of unease lingered. Rumors had begun to circulate about individuals and organizations with nefarious intentions, those who sought to exploit the power of the Eternal Echo for personal gain and control.

Emily had heard whispers of secret meetings and covert operations, and she couldn't shake the feeling that danger lurked in the shadows. She shared her concerns with Elizabeth and Daniel, who listened with grave expressions.

"We must be vigilant," Daniel said, his voice low. "The Eternal Echo is a powerful relic, and there are those who would stop at nothing to harness its capabilities."

Elizabeth nodded in agreement. "We cannot let our guard down. The responsibility of safeguarding the relic and its knowledge remains as crucial as ever."

Determined to protect the Eternal Echo, they devised a plan to enhance security measures within the consortium. They established a network of trusted individuals who would monitor any suspicious activity and ensure that the relic remained inaccessible to those who sought to misuse it.

But even as they took precautions, the echoes of danger continued to grow louder. It was during a late-night meeting in the consortium's headquarters that Emily first encountered evidence of a covert operation. She had been working late, reviewing ancient texts when she stumbled upon a hidden message encoded within one of the scrolls.

The message was cryptic, but its implications were clear—it hinted at a plot to steal the Eternal Echo and harness its power for unknown purposes. Emily's heart raced as she realized the gravity of the situation.

With trembling hands, she copied the message and hurriedly left the study room. She knew she had to share this discovery with Elizabeth and Daniel immediately. The echoes of danger had become a deafening roar, and the relic's safety was in jeopardy.

She found them in their shared office, their faces illuminated by the soft glow of lamplight as they pored over documents. Without preamble, Emily handed them the copied message and watched as their expressions darkened with concern.

"It seems our fears were not unfounded," Elizabeth said, her voice grim. "This message confirms that there is a plot to steal the Eternal Echo."

Daniel's jaw clenched as he read the message. "We must act swiftly. The relic's knowledge and power are too great to fall into the wrong hands."

They decided to convene an emergency meeting of the consortium, a gathering of scholars and historians who would discuss the threat and formulate a plan to protect the Eternal Echo. The urgency of the situation weighed heavily on them all, and the echoes of danger had drawn them together in a shared purpose.

The meeting took place in the grand hall of the National Archives, a cavernous space filled with rows of seats and a towering lectern at the front. The consortium members filed in, their expressions a mix of determination and apprehension.

Elizabeth and Daniel stood at the lectern, ready to address their colleagues. The room fell into silence as they recounted the discovery of the covert operation and the message that hinted at a plot to steal the relic.

"We cannot underestimate the danger we face," Daniel began, his voice resonating through the hall. "The Eternal Echo is a repository of knowledge and power that must be safeguarded at all costs. We are its custodians, and we bear the responsibility of protecting it from those who would misuse it."

Elizabeth continued, her gaze sweeping over the assembled scholars. "We have enhanced security measures, but we must remain vigilant. The threat is real, and we must be prepared to defend the relic with our lives, if necessary."

The consortium members nodded in agreement, their resolve unwavering. They understood the gravity of the situation, and they were prepared to do whatever it took to protect the Eternal Echo.

As the meeting continued, plans were set into motion. Security measures were tightened, and a network of informants was established to gather information on the covert operation. Every member of the consortium pledged their unwavering commitment to the relic's protection, and a sense of unity and purpose filled the hall.

But even as they prepared for the impending threat, Emily couldn't shake the feeling that there was more to the covert operation than met the eye. She had a nagging suspicion that the true nature of the danger went beyond the theft of the relic—it hinted at a larger, more sinister plot.

Driven by her curiosity and determination, Emily began to dig deeper, poring over ancient texts and manuscripts in search of clues. The more she uncovered, the more she became convinced that the danger extended far beyond the consortium's immediate concerns.

Late one night, as she delved into a particularly obscure manuscript, she stumbled upon a revelation that sent chills down her spine. It was a reference to a shadowy organization, one that had existed for centuries in the shadows, manipulating events and seeking to control the course of history.

The organization's name was whispered in hushed tones—The Order of the Obsidian Serpent. It was said to be a cabal of individuals with a singular purpose—to harness the power of the Eternal Echo and use it to reshape the world according to their own designs.

Emily knew that she had uncovered a dark secret, one that went beyond the immediate threat to the relic. The Order of the Obsidian Serpent posed a danger not only to the consortium but to the entire world. Their motives were shrouded in mystery, but their intentions were undoubtedly malevolent.

She shared her discovery with Elizabeth and Daniel, who listened with growing concern. It was clear that the threat they faced was far greater than they had initially realized.

"We must expose the Order and thwart their plans," Emily insisted, her voice determined. "The safety of the relic and the preservation of history depend on it."

Elizabeth and Daniel agreed, and they began to formulate a plan to unmask the Order of the Obsidian Serpent and put an end to their machinations. They knew that they could not do it alone—they would need the support of the consortium and the dedication of every member to succeed.

The consortium members gathered once more, this time with a renewed sense of purpose. Elizabeth, Daniel, and Emily shared the revelation of the Order of the Obsidian Serpent, explaining the extent of the danger that loomed over them.

"The Order is a formidable adversary," Elizabeth warned, her eyes scanning the determined faces of her colleagues. "But we have one advantage—the knowledge contained within the Eternal Echo. It has the power to reveal the truth and illuminate the darkest of secrets."

Daniel continued, "We must work together to uncover the Order's hidden members, their plans, and their motives. We are historians, scholars, and custodians of history. Let us use our knowledge to shine a light into the shadows and expose the truth."

The consortium members nodded in agreement, their commitment unwavering. They understood the gravity of the situation and the pivotal role they would play in the battle against the Order of the Obsidian Serpent.

The investigation into the Order's activities began in earnest. The consortium's informants worked tirelessly to gather information, while scholars delved into the relics' vast repository of knowledge, searching for clues and connections that might lead to the Order's members.

As days turned into weeks and weeks into months, the pieces of the puzzle slowly began to fall into place. The Order's network was vast and intricate, but it was not impenetrable. Gradually, the identities of key members were uncovered, and their motives began to emerge.

It became clear that the Order sought to manipulate history for their own gain, to rewrite the past and shape the future according to their designs. Their quest for power and control knew no bounds, and they were willing to use the Eternal Echo's knowledge to achieve their sinister goals.

The consortium members worked tirelessly to gather evidence against the Order, documenting their activities and exposing their hidden agendas. They knew that the battle against the Order was not only a fight for the relic's safety but a battle for the preservation of history itself.

But as they delved deeper into the investigation, they realized that the Order was not a monolithic entity—it was a web of factions and alliances, each with its own agenda and goals. Uniting against a common enemy would be a formidable challenge, but it was one they were willing to undertake.

Emily, driven by her determination to uncover the truth, played a pivotal role in exposing the Order's inner workings. She infiltrated their ranks, posing as a historian seeking to align with their goals. It was a dangerous gambit, one that required nerves of steel and a commitment to the cause.

She discovered that the Order had infiltrated various institutions and organizations, wielding their influence behind the scenes to further their agenda. They had spies and agents in positions of power, ready to manipulate events to their advantage.

But Emily was not alone in her efforts. Elizabeth, Daniel, and the consortium members provided her with support and guidance, ensuring her safety and the success of her mission. Together, they gathered the evidence needed to expose the Order's activities to the world.

The culmination of their efforts came during a dramatic confrontation at a clandestine meeting of the Order of the Obsidian Serpent. Emily, with her newfound knowledge and the support of the consortium, revealed the extent of their investigations and the evidence they had gathered.

The meeting room, shrouded in secrecy, became a battleground of words and revelations. The Order's members were shocked and angered by the exposure of their activities, their carefully crafted plans unraveling before their eyes.

As the truth was laid bare, the consortium members, along with law enforcement agencies, moved swiftly to apprehend the Order's key members. It was a coordinated effort that resulted in the arrest of individuals who had sought to manipulate history and reshape the world.

The world watched as the Order of the Obsidian Serpent was exposed and dismantled, its members held accountable for their actions. The revelations sent shockwaves through society, but they also served as a powerful reminder of the importance of preserving history and the dangers of those who would seek to rewrite it.

In the aftermath of the confrontation, the consortium members gathered once more, this time with a sense of triumph and closure. The threat to the Eternal Echo had been vanquished, and the relic's knowledge remained protected.

But their work was far from over. The preservation of history and the study of the Eternal Echo continued, as did the consortium's commitment to ensuring that the relic's power was used responsibly and ethically.

As they stood together, scholars and historians united by a shared purpose, they knew that their journey was ongoing. The echoes of danger had been silenced, but the echoes of history and the echoes of eternity would forever resonate in their hearts and minds.

Dr. Elizabeth Morgan, Professor Daniel Ramirez, and Emily Turner—protectors of the Eternal Echo and custodians of history—looked toward the future with a sense of hope and determination. Theirs was a legacy that transcended time, a legacy of knowledge, perseverance, and the unwavering belief that history held the key to understanding the present and shaping the future.

And so, the echoes continued to resonate, a reminder that history was not a static relic of the past but a living, breathing force that guided humanity on its journey through time.

Whispers of Destiny

The passage of time had been kind to Dr. Elizabeth Morgan, Professor Daniel Ramirez, and Emily Turner. Years had flowed like a gentle river, carrying with them the echoes of their past adventures and challenges. They had become pillars of the consortium, custodians of history, and guardians of the Eternal Echo.

On a crisp autumn morning, Elizabeth stood at the window of her study, gazing out at the golden leaves that danced in the breeze. The Eternal Echo, nestled securely within the National Archives, had become a beacon of enlightenment, drawing scholars and historians from around the world.

The relic's knowledge had continued to reveal hidden truths, and its power had been harnessed for the greater good. But the echoes of their past encounters with danger lingered in their minds, a reminder of the fragility of history and the relentless pursuit of those who would seek to manipulate it.

Emily had flourished as a historian, her dedication and determination leading her to become a respected scholar in her own right. She had taken up the mantle of leadership within the consortium, guiding its members in the responsible study of the Eternal Echo and the preservation of history.

Daniel, with his unwavering support, had become a renowned authority on ancient civilizations, his work shedding light on the mysteries of the past. Together, they had built a life filled with purpose and shared passion, their love enduring as strongly as ever.

But on this particular morning, as Elizabeth looked out at the changing season, a sense of restlessness stirred within her. It was as if the winds carried with them whispers of destiny, calling her to embark on a new adventure, one that would once again alter the course of their lives.

She turned away from the window, her gaze falling upon the portrait of the Whispering Grove that hung on her study wall. The ancient trees seemed to beckon to her, their branches reaching out like spectral fingers, urging her to listen to the echoes of eternity.

With a determined expression, she made her way to the consortium's meeting room, where Emily and Daniel were already gathered, their faces filled with curiosity at her unexpected summons.

"Something stirs within me," Elizabeth began, her voice filled with conviction. "I can't ignore the feeling that there's more to discover, more to understand about the Eternal Echo and the secrets it holds."

Emily nodded in agreement, her eyes shining with excitement. "I've felt it too, Elizabeth. There are still mysteries hidden within the relic, waiting to be uncovered."

Daniel, ever the voice of reason, spoke thoughtfully. "We've dedicated our lives to the preservation of history and the protection of the Eternal Echo. If there's a new adventure to be had, we should embark on it together."

And so, the decision was made. The three of them would set out on a new journey, one that would take them far from the familiar halls of the National Archives and into the unknown. The echoes of destiny had called, and they were ready to answer.

Their first destination was a remote village nestled deep within the Scottish Highlands, a place where ancient legends and mysteries held sway. It was said that the village was home to a hidden artifact—a companion piece to the Eternal Echo, known as the "Whispering Stone."

Legend had it that the Whispering Stone possessed the power to amplify the knowledge contained within the Eternal Echo, revealing even deeper insights into the past and the future. It was a relic of immense significance, and its existence had long been shrouded in myth and secrecy.

As they traveled to the village, their anticipation grew. The rugged landscape of the Highlands unfolded before them, its beauty and mystique a testament to the enduring power of nature. They could almost hear the whispers of the ancient stones, guiding them toward their destination.

Upon arriving in the village, they found themselves welcomed by the locals, who spoke of the legend of the Whispering Stone with a mixture of reverence and curiosity. It was said that the stone lay hidden within a nearby cave, a place of great importance to the village's history.

With the guidance of the villagers, they embarked on a treacherous journey through the Highland terrain, navigating winding paths and rocky cliffs. The echoes of their footsteps seemed to resonate with the whispers of destiny, guiding them toward their goal.

Finally, they arrived at the cave—a gaping maw in the side of a rugged hill. Its entrance was flanked by ancient standing stones, their carvings a testament to the people who had inhabited this land for generations.

As they ventured deeper into the cave, their torchlight revealed an otherworldly chamber. The walls were adorned with intricate symbols and carvings, and at its center lay the Whispering Stone—an ethereal, translucent gem that seemed to shimmer with hidden knowledge.

Elizabeth, Daniel, and Emily approached the stone with a sense of reverence. They could feel its power, a resonance that echoed with the Eternal Echo itself. It was as if the stone held the key to unlocking the relic's deepest secrets.

With trembling hands, Elizabeth reached out and touched the Whispering Stone. Instantly, her mind was flooded with images and insights—visions of civilizations long forgotten, prophecies of the future, and the mysteries of the cosmos.

She gasped, overwhelmed by the influx of knowledge. Her companions rushed to her side, their eyes wide with wonder. As she shared her revelations, they realized that the Whispering Stone had amplified the power of the Eternal Echo, opening a doorway to a realm of untold wisdom.

But the Whispering Stone was not without its challenges. Its power was a double-edged sword, capable of overwhelming the mind and distorting reality. As they delved deeper into its mysteries, they encountered visions and challenges that tested their resolve and their bond as a team.

In one vision, they found themselves in the midst of an ancient battle, witnessing the clash of armies and the fall of empires. In another, they glimpsed the future, a world transformed by the forces of nature and technology.

Each revelation brought with it a deeper understanding of the interconnectedness of history and the echoes of eternity. They realized that the relics were not just repositories of knowledge but gateways to a higher plane of existence, where past, present, and future converged.

As they emerged from the cave, their minds filled with the wisdom of the Whispering Stone, they knew that their journey was far from over. The echoes of destiny had guided them to this place, but their mission was not yet complete.

With the newfound knowledge of the Whispering Stone, they returned to the National Archives, their hearts filled with a sense of purpose and determination. The relic's power had been amplified, and the secrets it held were more profound than ever before.

But they also knew that their journey had only just begun. The echoes of destiny continued to whisper, leading them toward new adventures and challenges that awaited on the horizon. As custodians of history and guardians of the Eternal Echo, they were ready to embrace whatever the future held.

And so, Dr. Elizabeth Morgan, Professor Daniel Ramirez, and Emily Turner stood at the precipice of a new chapter in their lives, their hearts filled with the echoes of destiny and the boundless potential of the knowledge they held. The journey was ongoing, and they would continue to explore the mysteries of the past, the present, and the future, knowing that the echoes of eternity would always guide their way.

Back at the National Archives, Elizabeth, Daniel, and Emily set to work deciphering the wealth of knowledge they had gained from the Whispering Stone. The gem had not only amplified the power of the Eternal Echo but had also granted them deeper insights into the complexities of history and the interconnectedness of the world.

They spent days and nights poring over ancient texts and manuscripts, cross-referencing the newfound knowledge with the vast repository of the Eternal Echo. The revelations they uncovered were both awe-inspiring and humbling, revealing a tapestry of history that stretched far beyond their previous understanding.

One revelation that struck them deeply was the existence of a secret society known as the "Harbingers of Eternity." This society had existed for centuries, its members dedicated to preserving the knowledge contained within relics like the Eternal Echo and the Whispering Stone.

The Harbingers of Eternity believed that the relics held the key to humanity's survival and evolution, and they had worked covertly throughout history to safeguard these artifacts and the wisdom they contained. It was clear that their intentions aligned with the goals of the consortium—to protect and preserve the knowledge of the past.

As they continued to delve into the history of the Harbingers, they uncovered a series of encrypted messages and clues hidden within the Whispering Stone's revelations. It was as if the stone itself was guiding them toward a greater purpose, a mission that went beyond the preservation of knowledge.

One message, in particular, caught their attention—a cryptic reference to a place known as the "Echo Chamber." It was described as a sanctuary of wisdom, a place where the relics' power could be harnessed for the betterment of humanity.

Determined to uncover the truth, Elizabeth, Daniel, and Emily embarked on a new journey, following the clues provided by the Whispering Stone. Their quest led them to a remote monastery nestled high in the Himalayan mountains—a place of quiet contemplation and ancient wisdom.

The monks of the monastery welcomed them with a sense of recognition, as if they had been expecting their arrival. It became clear that the monks were the modern-day descendants of the Harbingers of Eternity, keepers of the Echo Chamber's secrets.

Inside the monastery, they discovered a chamber unlike any other—a place filled with relics of immense power, including an array of Whispering Stones and other artifacts connected to the Eternal Echo. The chamber resonated with a profound energy, as if the echoes of history and the whispers of destiny converged within its walls.

The monks explained that the Echo Chamber had been created as a sanctuary of wisdom, a place where the relics' power could be harnessed and used for the betterment of humanity. It was a place of meditation and revelation, where individuals could connect with the collective knowledge of the past, present, and future.

But the true purpose of the Echo Chamber went even deeper. It was revealed that the relics possessed a hidden potential—a power that could bring about a profound transformation in the world. The monks believed that, when harnessed responsibly, the relics had the ability to heal divisions, promote understanding, and guide humanity toward a more enlightened future.

Elizabeth, Daniel, and Emily realized that they were standing at the threshold of a new era—a time when the relics' power could be used to bridge gaps in knowledge and understanding, to illuminate the darkest corners of history, and to inspire a sense of unity among people from all walks of life.

With the guidance of the monks, they began to explore the Echo Chamber's capabilities. They connected with the relics on a deeper level, allowing the echoes of history and destiny to flow through them. It was as if they had become conduits of knowledge, vessels through which the relics' power could be channeled.

As they immersed themselves in the relics' power, they began to experience visions—visions of a world where history was not a source of division but a bridge to understanding, where the echoes of eternity guided humanity toward a brighter future.

It was during one such vision that they saw the potential for a global consortium—an alliance of scholars, historians, and custodians of history from every corner of the world. This consortium would be dedicated to the responsible study and preservation of relics like the Eternal Echo and the Whispering Stone, using their power to promote peace, understanding, and the advancement of knowledge.

The vision filled them with a sense of purpose and determination. They knew that the time had come to share their discoveries with the world, to unite scholars and historians in a common cause, and to harness the relics' power for the greater good.

With the blessings of the monks, they returned to the National Archives, where they gathered the consortium members and shared their vision. The response was overwhelmingly positive, and scholars from around the world pledged their support to the cause.

The Global Consortium of Relic Custodians was born—a coalition of individuals dedicated to the responsible study and preservation of relics of historical significance. The consortium's mission was clear—to use the relics' power to promote understanding, bridge divides, and guide humanity toward a more enlightened future.

The echoes of destiny had led them to this moment, a moment when the relics' power could be harnessed for the betterment of humanity. Elizabeth, Daniel, and Emily stood at the forefront of this new era, custodians of history and champions of knowledge.

As they looked toward the future, they knew that their journey was far from over. The echoes of eternity would continue to guide them, revealing new mysteries, and shaping the course of history. But they were ready, united by a shared purpose and the belief that the relics held the key to a brighter and more enlightened world.

And so, the story of Dr. Elizabeth Morgan, Professor Daniel Ramirez, and Emily Turner continued, a tale of discovery, determination, and the enduring power of the echoes of destiny. Their legacy would echo through the ages, a testament to the potential of knowledge and the unwavering belief that history could be a force for good in the world.

The Relics Awaken

The Global Consortium of Relic Custodians had grown in influence and reach, uniting scholars, historians, and custodians of history from every corner of the world. Under the guidance of Dr. Elizabeth Morgan, Professor Daniel Ramirez, and Emily Turner, the consortium had become a force for good, using the relics' power to promote understanding and enlightenment.

The relics, including the Eternal Echo and the Whispering Stone, had been brought to the consortium's headquarters, where they were carefully preserved and studied. The echoes of destiny continued to resonate, guiding their efforts and revealing new revelations about the past, present, and future.

But the relics held a power that had yet to be fully harnessed—a power that went beyond the amplification of knowledge. It was a power that had the potential to bring about a transformation, not just in the understanding of history, but in the very fabric of reality itself.

One fateful day, as Elizabeth, Daniel, and Emily stood before the relics, they experienced a profound shift in consciousness. It was as if the relics themselves had awakened, their power surging through the room, filling it with a vibrant energy.

The relics had become more than mere artifacts—they had become sentient beings, guardians of knowledge and wisdom, and bearers of a mission that went beyond the boundaries of time.

"We've reached a pivotal moment," Daniel whispered, his eyes filled with wonder. "The relics have awakened to a higher purpose, a purpose that goes beyond our understanding."

Emily nodded, her heart pounding with excitement. "It's as if they're calling us to embark on a new adventure, one that will unlock their true potential."

Elizabeth, their leader and guide, felt a deep sense of responsibility. "We must heed the relics' call and discover their purpose. They have the power to reshape the world, and we must ensure that their power is used for the greater good."

With their minds connected to the relics, they experienced visions—visions of a world where the relics' power had transformed society, where the echoes of history and destiny guided humanity toward a brighter future. It was a world where knowledge was a force for unity, understanding, and enlightenment.

Determined to uncover the relics' true purpose, they embarked on a new journey, traveling to a hidden sanctuary known as the "Temple of Resonance." This ancient temple, shrouded in mystery and legend, was said to be a place where the relics' power could be harnessed and channeled for a greater purpose.

As they entered the temple, they were greeted by an ethereal glow—a radiant energy that filled the air and resonated with the relics' power. It was as if the very stones of the temple were infused with the wisdom of the ages.

Deep within the temple, they discovered a chamber unlike any other. At its center lay a pedestal, upon which rested a relic of immense significance—a crystal known as the "Heart of Resonance."

The Heart of Resonance pulsed with a rhythmic energy, its light dancing like a living heartbeat. It was the key to unlocking the relics' true potential, a conduit through which their power could be harnessed and directed.

With reverence, Elizabeth, Daniel, and Emily approached the crystal. As they touched it, they felt a surge of energy flow through them, connecting them to the relics and to each other in a profound way.

Visions filled their minds—visions of a world where the relics' power was used to bridge divides, to heal wounds, and to promote understanding among all people. It was a world where the echoes of history and destiny guided humanity toward a future of unity and enlightenment.

Realizing the enormity of their mission, they understood that the relics' power could not be kept hidden away. It had to be shared with the world, used to bring about a transformation in society, and to guide humanity toward a brighter future.

With the Heart of Resonance as their guide, they returned to the consortium's headquarters, where they shared their discoveries with the members. The response was overwhelming, and scholars from around the world pledged their support to the cause.

The relics' power was channeled through the Heart of Resonance, creating a network of knowledge and enlightenment that spanned the globe. It was a force for unity, a beacon of understanding, and a catalyst for positive change.

But they also knew that their mission was not without challenges. There were those who sought to exploit the relics' power for personal gain or to further their own agendas. The relics had enemies, individuals and organizations that would stop at nothing to control their power.

In the shadows, a new threat had emerged—an organization known as the "Seekers of Dominion." These individuals believed that the relics' power should be used to manipulate reality itself, to reshape the world according to their own desires.

The Seekers of Dominion were a formidable adversary, and they posed a danger not only to the consortium but to the very fabric of reality. Their motives were shrouded in darkness, and their actions threatened to destabilize the balance of knowledge and power.

Elizabeth, Daniel, and Emily realized that they could not face this threat alone. They needed allies—individuals who shared their commitment to the relics' true purpose and who were willing to stand against the forces of manipulation and control.

With the Heart of Resonance as their guide, they reached out to like-minded individuals from every corner of the world. Scholars, historians, and custodians of history from diverse backgrounds and cultures joined their cause, forming a coalition known as the "Harmony Keepers."

The Harmony Keepers were dedicated to the responsible use of the relics' power, to promoting understanding and unity among all people, and to thwarting the plans of the Seekers of Dominion.

As the two factions clashed in a battle of ideologies and power, the relics themselves began to resonate with a force greater than ever before. The Heart of Resonance pulsed with an energy that could not be denied, connecting the Harmony Keepers and the relics in a profound way.

In a climactic confrontation, the Harmony Keepers and the Seekers of Dominion faced off, their actions determining the fate of the relics and the course of history itself. It was a battle of ideals, a clash of forces that would shape the destiny of humanity.

As the relics' power surged through the Heart of Resonance, the Harmony Keepers stood united, their resolve unshakeable. They understood that the relics held the key to a better future, a future where knowledge and understanding could guide humanity toward enlightenment.

In the end, the Seekers of Dominion were defeated, their dark ambitions thwarted by the united efforts of the Harmony Keepers. The relics' power was preserved, and their true purpose was realized—a purpose that went beyond the amplification of knowledge and into the realm of transformation.

The echoes of destiny had led them to this moment, a moment when the relics' power was used to bring about positive change in the world. Elizabeth, Daniel, and Emily stood at the forefront of this new era, custodians of history and champions of knowledge.

As they looked toward the future, they knew that their journey was far from over. The relics' power continued to resonate, their potential to transform society and guide humanity toward enlightenment a force that could not be denied.

And so, the story of Dr. Elizabeth Morgan, Professor Daniel Ramirez, and Emily Turner continued, a tale of discovery, determination, and the enduring power of the relics and the echoes of destiny. Their legacy would echo through the ages, a testament to the potential of knowledge and the unwavering belief that history could be a force for good in the world.

The Harmony Keepers, united by their commitment to the relics' true purpose, worked tirelessly to promote understanding and enlightenment on a global scale. The relics' power became a beacon of hope, guiding humanity toward a brighter future.

As the years passed, the consortium's headquarters expanded, becoming a center for knowledge and diplomacy. Scholars, historians, and leaders from all corners of the world came together to exchange ideas, to learn from the past, and to build a future based on unity and cooperation.

The relics themselves continued to reveal hidden truths and insights into the mysteries of history. The Eternal Echo, with its timeless knowledge, became a source of inspiration for generations of scholars. The Whispering Stone, with its ability to amplify understanding, played a crucial role in resolving conflicts and fostering diplomacy among nations.

But the relics also served as a reminder of the importance of responsible stewardship. The Harmony Keepers remained vigilant, guarding against those who would seek to misuse the relics' power for personal gain or to sow discord.

As the echoes of destiny guided them forward, Elizabeth, Daniel, and Emily watched as the world changed around them. The relics' influence had a profound impact, bringing about a renaissance of knowledge and understanding.

In a world once divided by ignorance and prejudice, the relics helped to bridge gaps and promote empathy among people of diverse backgrounds and cultures. The echoes of history became a unifying force, reminding humanity of its shared heritage and interconnectedness.

The relics' power also had a tangible impact on society. Scientific and technological advancements flourished, fueled by a deepening understanding of the past and a commitment to using knowledge for the betterment of all.

In a world facing complex challenges, from environmental crises to political conflicts, the relics served as a guiding light. The Harmony Keepers, with their unwavering dedication, worked tirelessly to find solutions rooted in wisdom and compassion.

As the years turned into decades and the decades into centuries, the relics and the Harmony Keepers became legends in their own right. Their story was passed down through generations, a tale of heroes who had harnessed the power of history to shape a brighter future.

And so, the echoes of destiny continued to resonate, guiding humanity toward a future where knowledge, understanding, and unity were cherished above all else. Dr. Elizabeth Morgan, Professor Daniel Ramirez, and Emily Turner had embarked on a journey that transcended time, leaving an indelible mark on the course of history itself.

Their legacy lived on in the hearts and minds of those who believed in the power of the relics and the echoes of destiny. In a world filled with challenges and uncertainties, they remained a beacon of hope, a reminder that the pursuit of knowledge and the preservation of history could lead to a future filled with light and enlightenment.

And as long as the relics endured and the Harmony Keepers remained vigilant, the echoes of destiny would continue to guide humanity on its timeless journey through the ages.

The Echoes Resonate

Years had passed since the Harmony Keepers had united to harness the power of the relics and promote understanding and enlightenment in the world. The relics—the Eternal Echo and the Whispering Stone—had become revered symbols of wisdom and unity, their influence spreading far and wide.

Dr. Elizabeth Morgan, Professor Daniel Ramirez, and Emily Turner, now in the twilight of their years, had continued to guide the consortium and the Harmony Keepers. Their unwavering commitment to the relics' true purpose had left an indelible mark on the world.

One crisp autumn morning, as Elizabeth stood before the Eternal Echo, she felt a peculiar sensation—an echo of a different kind. It was as if the relics themselves were trying to convey a message, a call to action that went beyond their previous understanding.

She turned to her companions, her eyes filled with curiosity. "Have either of you felt something… unusual?"

Daniel and Emily exchanged glances before nodding in agreement. They too had sensed a shift in the relics' energy, a resonance that seemed to be calling them to a new adventure.

"It's as if the relics are trying to tell us something," Emily mused, her voice tinged with excitement. "A new chapter in our journey, perhaps?"

Elizabeth nodded, her heart filled with anticipation. "Let's follow the echoes and see where they lead us."

With their minds connected to the relics, they experienced visions—visions of a place shrouded in mist and mystery. It was a remote island, known as the "Isle of Echoes," a place of ancient legend and untold secrets.

The echoes of destiny had led them to this enigmatic island, where the relics' power seemed to resonate with a force stronger than ever before. They knew that their journey was far from over, and that the relics had a new purpose to reveal.

As they set foot on the Isle of Echoes, they were greeted by a landscape unlike any other. The mist that shrouded the island seemed to whisper secrets of the past, and the air was filled with a sense of anticipation.

Their exploration led them to a hidden cavern, deep within the heart of the island. Inside the cavern, they discovered a chamber adorned with ancient carvings and symbols—a chamber that seemed to pulse with the relics' power.

At the center of the chamber stood a pedestal, upon which rested a relic of astonishing beauty—a crystal known as the "Resonance Orb." The orb radiated a vibrant energy, and its light danced like a symphony of colors.

With reverence, Elizabeth, Daniel, and Emily approached the Resonance Orb. As they touched it, they felt a surge of energy flow through them, connecting them to the relics and to each other in a profound way.

Visions filled their minds—visions of a world where the relics' power was used to heal, to bring about unity among nations, and to guide humanity toward a future of unparalleled enlightenment. It was a world where the echoes of history and destiny resonated in perfect harmony.

Realizing the significance of their discovery, they understood that the relics' power was evolving, taking on a new purpose. The Resonance Orb was the key to unlocking this new potential, a potential that could reshape the world in profound ways.

With the Resonance Orb as their guide, they returned to the consortium's headquarters, where they shared their findings with the members. The response was filled with awe and excitement, and scholars from around the world pledged their support to the cause.

The relics' power, now channeled through the Resonance Orb, created a network of knowledge and unity that spanned the globe. It was a force for healing, for understanding, and for fostering cooperation among nations.

But they also knew that their mission faced challenges. There were those who would seek to exploit the relics' power for their own gain or to sow discord among nations. The relics had enemies, individuals and organizations that would stop at nothing to control their newfound potential.

In the shadows, a new threat had emerged—an organization known as the "Eclipse Conclave." These individuals believed that the relics' power should be used to manipulate reality itself, to reshape the world according to their own desires.

The Eclipse Conclave were a formidable adversary, and they posed a danger not only to the consortium but to the very fabric of reality. Their motives were shrouded in darkness, and their actions threatened to disrupt the balance of knowledge and power.

Elizabeth, Daniel, and Emily realized that they could not face this threat alone. They needed allies—individuals who shared their commitment to the relics' true purpose and who were willing to stand against the forces of manipulation and control.

With the Resonance Orb as their guide, they reached out to like-minded individuals from every corner of the world. Scholars, historians, and custodians of history from diverse backgrounds and cultures joined their cause, forming a coalition known as the "Harmony Resonators."

The Harmony Resonators were dedicated to the responsible use of the relics' power, to promoting healing and unity among nations, and to thwarting the plans of the Eclipse Conclave.

As the two factions clashed in a battle of ideologies and power, the relics themselves began to resonate with a force greater than ever before. The Resonance Orb pulsed with an energy that could not be denied, connecting the Harmony Resonators and the relics in a profound way.

In a climactic confrontation, the Harmony Resonators and the Eclipse Conclave faced off, their actions determining the fate of the relics and the course of reality itself. It was a battle of ideals, a clash of forces that would shape the destiny of humanity.

As the relics' power surged through the Resonance Orb, the Harmony Resonators stood united, their resolve unshakeable. They understood that the relics held the key to a better future, a future where knowledge, understanding, and unity could guide humanity toward enlightenment.

In the end, the Eclipse Conclave were defeated, their dark ambitions thwarted by the united efforts of the Harmony Resonators. The relics' power, now harnessed through the Resonance Orb, was preserved, and their new purpose was realized—a purpose that went beyond the amplification of knowledge and into the realm of transformation.

The echoes of destiny had led them to this moment, a moment when the relics' power was used to bring about positive change in the world. Elizabeth, Daniel, and Emily stood at the forefront of this new era, custodians of history and champions of a brighter future.

As they looked toward the future, they knew that their journey was far from over. The relics' power continued to resonate, their potential to heal and transform reality a force that could not be denied.

And so, the story of Dr. Elizabeth Morgan, Professor Daniel Ramirez, and Emily Turner continued, a tale of discovery, determination, and the enduring power of the relics and the echoes of destiny. Their legacy lived on in the hearts and minds of those who believed in the potential of knowledge and the unwavering belief that history could be a force for healing and transformation in the world.

As long as the relics endured and the Harmony Resonators remained vigilant, the echoes of destiny would continue to guide humanity on its timeless journey through the ages, resonating in harmony with the forces of light and enlightenment.

The Symphony of Resonance

The years had been kind to the Harmony Resonators, and the world had thrived under their stewardship of the relics and the Resonance Orb. The echoes of destiny had guided humanity toward an era of unprecedented enlightenment, understanding, and unity.

Dr. Elizabeth Morgan, Professor Daniel Ramirez, and Emily Turner, now wise elders, continued to lead the consortium and the Harmony Resonators. Their shared dedication to the relics' true purpose had shaped a world where knowledge was a force for healing and transformation.

But as the decades passed, they couldn't help but feel a growing sense of urgency. The relics had revealed much, but there was still an uncharted realm of knowledge, a final revelation that remained tantalizingly out of reach.

One evening, as they gathered in the consortium's headquarters, a shimmering resonance filled the air. The Resonance Orb glowed with a brilliance they had never seen before, and its colors shifted and danced in an intricate pattern.

Elizabeth, her eyes wide with wonder, whispered, "It's as if the Resonance Orb is trying to tell us something—something important."

Daniel nodded, his face etched with curiosity. "I've never seen it behave like this before. It's as if it's inviting us to explore a new dimension of knowledge."

Emily, her heart racing, said, "Let's follow the resonance and discover what lies beyond."

With their minds connected to the relics and the Resonance Orb, they experienced visions—visions of a hidden realm, a place known as the "Chamber of Cosmic Resonance." It was a dimension of existence that transcended time and space, a place where the echoes of destiny resonated with unparalleled power.

They understood that their journey had reached its most pivotal moment yet. The Chamber of Cosmic Resonance held the key to the relics' ultimate purpose, a purpose that could reshape not only the world but the very fabric of the universe itself.

As they embarked on this new adventure, they were filled with a sense of awe and trepidation. The path to the Chamber was shrouded in mystery, and its entrance lay hidden in a realm beyond the reach of ordinary mortals.

Their journey took them to the farthest reaches of the world, to ancient temples, sacred mountains, and hidden caves. Along the way, they encountered challenges and trials that tested their resolve and deepened their connection to the relics and the Resonance Orb.

At last, after a quest that spanned years, they stood before the entrance to the Chamber of Cosmic Resonance. Its walls seemed to shimmer with energy, and the echoes of destiny filled the air with a haunting melody.

With trepidation and reverence, they entered the chamber, and what they beheld left them breathless. The chamber was a vast expanse of pulsating energy, filled with swirling patterns of light and sound. It was a symphony of resonance, a dance of cosmic forces beyond mortal comprehension.

At the heart of the chamber stood a structure that defied description—a crystalline portal, known as the "Nexus of Eternity," that connected the relics, the Resonance Orb, and the very essence of existence itself.

As they approached the Nexus, they felt an overwhelming surge of energy. Visions and revelations washed over them, revealing the true purpose of the relics and the Resonance Orb.

The relics were not merely vessels of knowledge—they were keys to unlocking the harmony of the cosmos, to tapping into the universal resonance that bound all things together. The Resonance Orb was the conduit through which this cosmic harmony could be harnessed and directed.

The Chamber of Cosmic Resonance held the power to heal not only the divisions among nations but the very fractures in the fabric of the universe. It was a place where the echoes of destiny and the symphony of existence converged, offering the means to restore balance and harmony on a cosmic scale.

Elizabeth, her voice filled with awe, said, "This is the revelation we've been seeking all these years—a revelation that goes beyond our world and into the very heart of the cosmos."

Daniel, his eyes shining with understanding, added, "The relics and the Resonance Orb are not just tools of knowledge; they are instruments of cosmic resonance. They hold the power to heal and transform the universe itself."

Emily, her heart filled with determination, said, "We must use this power responsibly, to restore balance and harmony to the cosmos. It is a sacred duty that we cannot ignore."

With newfound purpose and resolve, they channeled the cosmic resonance through the relics and the Resonance Orb. The energy flowed through them, connecting them to the very essence of existence.

As they did so, the Nexus of Eternity pulsed with a radiant light, and a wave of cosmic harmony spread outward, touching every corner of the universe. The fractures in the fabric of existence began to mend, and the echoes of destiny resonated with a sublime melody that filled the cosmos with unity and understanding.

The Chamber of Cosmic Resonance had served its purpose, and as they left its shimmering depths, they knew that their journey was far from over. The relics, now imbued with the power of cosmic resonance, would continue to guide them toward a future where knowledge, understanding, and unity would reign supreme.

Back at the consortium's headquarters, they shared their revelations with the members, who pledged their support to the cause of cosmic harmony. The relics and the Resonance Orb became symbols of hope and transformation, and their influence extended beyond the boundaries of Earth to touch the farthest reaches of the universe.

The echoes of destiny had led them to this moment, a moment when the relics' power was used to restore balance and harmony on a cosmic scale. Elizabeth, Daniel, and Emily stood at the forefront of a new era, custodians of history and champions of cosmic resonance.

As they looked toward the future, they knew that their journey was boundless. The relics and the Resonance Orb held the key to a universe where knowledge, understanding, and unity were cherished above all else.

And so, the story of Dr. Elizabeth Morgan, Professor Daniel Ramirez, and Emily Turner continued, a tale of discovery, determination, and the enduring power of the relics, the Resonance Orb, and the cosmic symphony of resonance. Their legacy lived on in the hearts and minds of all beings, a testament to the potential of knowledge and the unwavering belief that history could be a force for healing and transformation in the cosmos.

As long as the relics endured and the Harmony Resonators remained vigilant, the echoes of destiny and the cosmic symphony of resonance would continue to guide the universe on its timeless journey toward a future where the power of knowledge and understanding would always triumph over darkness and discord.

The Symphony's Legacy

The years passed, and the world continued to bask in the harmony brought about by the cosmic resonance channeled through the relics and the Resonance Orb. Humanity thrived, and the universe itself resonated with newfound balance and understanding.

Dr. Elizabeth Morgan, Professor Daniel Ramirez, and Emily Turner, now venerable figures in the consortium and among the Harmony Resonators, watched with pride as their legacy unfolded. The relics and the Resonance Orb had become symbols of hope and transformation, revered by all.

However, there was one final revelation—a revelation that would complete their journey and secure the future of cosmic harmony. The relics had been instruments of transformation, but they held yet another secret—a secret that would bring their mission full circle.

One evening, as they gathered in the consortium's headquarters, they sensed a profound resonance in the air. The Relics and the Resonance Orb pulsed with a gentle light, and the echoes of destiny whispered a tantalizing message.

Emily, her eyes alight with curiosity, said, "It's as if the relics are trying to communicate something new, something we haven't yet comprehended."

Daniel nodded, his brows furrowed in thought. "Perhaps it's time to unlock the final layer of their power, the culmination of our journey."

Elizabeth, her heart filled with anticipation, said, "Let's follow the echoes one last time and see where they lead us."

With their minds connected to the relics and the Resonance Orb, they experienced visions—visions of a place beyond time and space, a realm known as the "Symphony of Eternity." It was a dimension where the echoes of destiny, the cosmic resonance, and the relics converged in perfect harmony.

They understood that their ultimate destination lay in the Symphony of Eternity, a place where the true purpose of the relics and the Resonance Orb would be revealed. It was a journey that would require the deepest understanding and the most profound wisdom.

Their quest led them on a path that transcended physical boundaries. They traversed the very fabric of existence, moving through realms beyond human comprehension. Along the way, they encountered challenges and tests of their unwavering commitment to the relics' mission.

After a journey that spanned time and space, they arrived at the threshold of the Symphony of Eternity. It was a place of indescribable beauty, where colors and sounds merged into a celestial symphony that resonated with the heartbeat of the cosmos.

In the heart of the Symphony stood the "Conductor's Baton," a crystalline artifact of unparalleled significance. It radiated a harmonious energy that transcended time and space, and its resonance was the source of the cosmic symphony that bound the universe together.

As they approached the Conductor's Baton, they felt a profound connection to the relics and the Resonance Orb, and the echoes of destiny filled their minds with a revelation that left them awestruck.

The relics and the Resonance Orb were not just instruments of cosmic harmony—they were the key to conducting the Symphony of Eternity itself. They held the power to shape the very destiny of the cosmos, to guide it toward a future of eternal balance and understanding.

Elizabeth, her voice filled with reverence, said, "This is the final revelation we've been seeking—the ultimate purpose of the relics and the Resonance Orb. We are the conductors of the cosmic symphony."

Daniel, his eyes shining with understanding, added, "Our role is to ensure that the universe remains in perfect harmony, to use the relics and the Resonance Orb to guide it toward eternal enlightenment."

Emily, her heart filled with determination, said, "We must accept this sacred duty and conduct the Symphony of Eternity with wisdom and compassion."

With the Conductor's Baton in hand, they channeled their collective energy into the relics and the Resonance Orb, becoming the conductors of the cosmic symphony. As they did so, the Symphony of Eternity pulsed with a radiant light, and the universe itself responded to their guidance.

The cosmic symphony resonated with newfound harmony, filling every corner of existence with unity and understanding. The echoes of destiny merged into a sublime melody that transcended time and space, connecting all beings in the universe.

The relics, the Resonance Orb, and the Conductor's Baton had fulfilled their ultimate purpose, and the legacy of the Harmony Resonators was secured. Humanity and the cosmos itself would forever thrive in a state of eternal balance and enlightenment.

Back at the consortium's headquarters, they shared their revelations with the members, who pledged their support to the continued stewardship of the relics and the cosmic symphony. The relics and the Resonance Orb became the instruments of eternal enlightenment, guiding the universe toward a future where harmony reigned supreme.

The echoes of destiny had led them to this moment, a moment when the relics' power was used to conduct the Symphony of Eternity itself. Elizabeth, Daniel, and Emily stood at the forefront of a new era, the eternal conductors of cosmic harmony.

As they looked toward the future, they knew that their journey was timeless. The relics, the Resonance Orb, and the cosmic symphony held the key to a universe where knowledge, understanding, and unity were cherished above all else.

And so, the story of Dr. Elizabeth Morgan, Professor Daniel Ramirez, and Emily Turner reached its majestic crescendo, a tale of discovery, determination, and the enduring power of the relics, the Resonance Orb, and the Symphony of Eternity. Their legacy lived on in the hearts and minds of all beings, a testament to the potential of knowledge and the unwavering belief that history could be a force for eternal harmony in the cosmos.

As long as the relics endured, and the conductors of the Symphony remained vigilant, the echoes of destiny and the cosmic symphony of eternity would continue to guide the universe on its timeless journey toward a future where the power of knowledge and understanding would forever be in perfect harmony.

www.ingramcontent.com/pod-product-compliance
Lightning Source LLC
LaVergne TN
LVHW050026080526
838202LV00069B/6923